THIS BOOK
BELONGS TO

Mariella Mouse in the Opera House

First edition ©2014 Dottie Withrow. All rights reserved

No part of this book may be reproduced in any form without written permission from the author, except for the inclusion of brief quotations/reviews.

Library of Congress Catalog Number:

ISBN-13: 978-0-615-77749-8

Published by Dottie Withrow, Florida
Illustrations by Robert Brent
Design and layout by Infinity Graphics

For my grandchildren

iv

Mariella Mouse lives in a house with an old man and an old woman. She has her very own cozy nest under the floor right next to the kitchen door.

It is a perfect place for Mariella to see everything and hear everything.

1

Mozart Mouse lives in the house with the old man and old woman. He lives in the attic.

From there,
Mozart can peek down the stairs into the kitchen where he can see everything and hear everything.

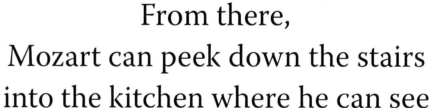

Each morning
Mariella and Mozart
skitter into the kitchen.

2

Each morning the radio,
sitting on the cabinet shelf,
plays beautiful opera music.

The old man bakes a loaf of bread for supper
and sings in his beautiful low voice.

The old woman stirs a pot
of soup for supper and sings
along in her beautiful high voice.

When the music is over,
they look at each other
and exclaim "I love Aida.
I love La Bohème.
Remember when....?"

For Mariella and Mozart, mornings are, indeed,
wonderful in the little house. Afternoons are perfect as well.

It is concert time in the little house. The old man plays the piano.
The old woman stands beside him. And again, the old man
and old woman sing the beautiful arias from their favorite operas.

Mariella squeals,
"I love it! I love it!"
in her noisiest voice.

"Hush!"
whispers Mozart.
"We are the audience
and we must be
on our best behavior."

"There will be a time later
for clapping and shouting
BRAVO."

Mornings are wonderful
in the little house.
Afternoons are perfect.
But evenings are mysterious.

After their supper
of soup and bread,
the old man
and old woman
put on their coats
and hurry out the door.

6

The house feels very empty.
The house feels very quiet.

There are no voices
singing beautiful arias.

Mozart returns
to his nest in the attic.

Mariella crawls
into her nest
near the kitchen door
and falls fast asleep.

Every day, the old man and old woman bake bread, stir soup, and sing.
Every day, the piano is played and the arias are sung.
Every day, Mariella and Mozart are very happy
listening to the beautiful music.

But Mariella and Mozart wonder where the old man and old woman are going every evening.

9

Finally, Mozart
decides to
take matters
into his own paws.

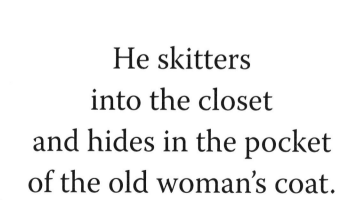

He skitters
into the closet
and hides in the pocket
of the old woman's coat.

He snuggles down and lies very still, and before long,
finds himself transported to a large stone building.
The sign over the door says OPERA HOUSE.

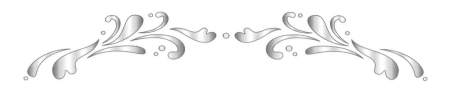

"Oh my goodness!" squeals Mozart.
"Mariella will never believe where I am!
The old man and old woman
have come to the Opera House!"

"I love Aida," Mozart whispers to himself.
"I love La Bohème."

The next morning, Mariella comes to the kitchen
to watch the old woman stir soup
and the old man bake bread.

She listens to them sing
in their beautiful voices.

But Mozart
does not appear
in the kitchen.

Nor does he appear
in the afternoon
for concert time.

Mariella is worried
and lonely.

"Oh my!
Where could Mozart be?"

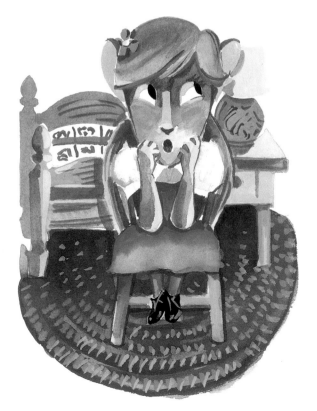

15

Mariella decides
to take matters
into her own paws.

So she skitters
out the door.

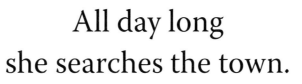

All day long
she searches the town.
When the moon and stars come out,
Mariella continues her search.
She searches long
into the night.

As the sun rises in the morning sky,
Mariella comes upon a large stone building.
Lanterns still light the walkway.
Over the door are the words

OPERA HOUSE

Mariella creeps inside and finds herself facing a stage,
an orchestra pit, and lots of seats.

"Oh my goodness!" squeals Mariella.
"Mozart will never believe where I am!
This must be the Grand Tier of the Opera House."

Mariella
is very tired,
so she finds
a small space
under the floor.
"I think I shall
be most
comfortable
here,"
she whispers
to herself.

Mariella
falls
fast
asleep.

Suddenly, Mariella is awakened by a loud noise.
There are people everywhere,
moving boxes and sweeping floors.

21

Then she sees a strange sight:

A large man
walks through the door
and onto the stage.
Beside him is a
large spotted dog.

"Good morning, everyone.
I brought my dog,
Tchaikovsky, with me today,"
the large man sings
in his low Bass voice.

"Oh dear!" squeals Mariella.
"I cannot believe my eyes.
Why would anyone bring such a
huge dog into the Opera House?"

Before Mariella can take refuge
in her cozy nest, the door opens again
and Mariella sees another strange sight.

Another man walks
on to the stage.
Beside him is another dog.

"Good morning, everyone.
I brought my dog, Verdi, with me today,"
the man sings in his Baritone voice.

"Another dog!"
gasps Mariella.

And before Mariella
can dive for cover,
a parrot flies
through the door.

A third man
walks onto the stage.
"Good morning, everyone.
In case you hadn't noticed,
I brought my parrot,
Donizetti, with me today,"
he sings in his Tenor voice.

Mariella shakes with fright.

24

But the door opens again.
Two women walk in.
"Good morning, everyone,"
sings the Mezzo Soprano
in her medium voice.
"Please meet my cats,
Puccini I and Puccini II."

"Good morning everyone,"
sings the Lyric Soprano
in her very high voice.
"Please meet my cat, Rossini."

"Oh my!" squeals Mariella.
"The Opera House
is getting very crowded."

All day long, the animals behave very badly.
The dogs chase the cats. The cats chase the dogs.
The parrot swoops and squawks.
"Oh dear!" squeals Mariella.

"This is not a place for barking and chasing
and hissing and swooping and squawking."

26

27

"If Mozart were here, he would say, 'Hush! No Meows, no Woofs, no Arfs, no Squawks! You must be on your best behavior in the Opera House.'"

29

Then it is evening.
Mariella creeps into the Grand Tier of the Opera House.
She sees the stage and the lights.
She sees musicians in the orchestra pit.

She sees people coming into this beautiful performance space.

To her surprise, she sees a couple walk through the door.

Mariella cannot believe her eyes!

She recognizes them instantly—it is the old man and the old woman!

Now Mariella knows where the old man and the old woman
go each evening. They come to the Opera House!
Mystery solved.

Mariella
takes her seat
in the beautiful
performance space.

The houselights dim.
The curtain rises.
The conductor
raises his baton.
The orchestra begins playing
beautiful music.

Beautiful voices sing beautiful arias.
It sounds like the music in the little house.

Mariella hears the old man whisper,
"I love beautiful music. Remember when...?"
The old woman whispers, "I love beautiful arias.
Remember when...?"

And Mariella squeals in her noisiest voice, "I love it! I love it!"

"Hush!" whispers Mozart.
"We are the audience and we must be on our best behavior.
There will be a time later for clapping and shouting *BRAVO*."

What a surprise! There, beside her, is Mariella's favorite friend.
Mozart found. Mystery solved.

"What a perfect evening!"
exclaims Mariella.

"The old man and old woman are here.
Mozart Mouse is here.
Even the animals are here.
The dog, Tchaikovsky, is sitting quietly.
The dog, Verdi, is sitting quietly.
The cats, Puccini I, Puccini II,
and Rossini, are purring quietly.
And Donizetti, the parrot,
has the best seat in the Opera House.

Everyone is on their best behavior,
and everyone is listening."

BRAVO!

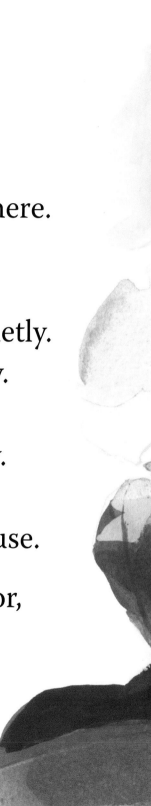

36

The End

TEACHABLE MOMENTS
from Mariella Mouse in the Opera House

TEACHABLE MOMENT 1
Everyone in the story loves music. They really love opera. What is an opera? How is it different from other plays?

TEACHABLE MOMENT 2
How do you know that the old man and old woman love Opera? How do you know that Mariella and Mozart love Opera?

TEACHABLE MOMENT 3
Rather than reading a story, have you ever sung a story? Did you like singing it?

TEACHABLE MOMENT 4
Have you ever gone to a large concert hall to watch a play or a musical program? Did you sit quietly and watch the program? Did you shout "BRAVO"?

TEACHABLE MOMENT 5
What is a mystery? How did Mozart decide to solve the mystery about where the old man and old woman were going?"

TEACHABLE MOMENT 6
Mariella searched for Mozart for a very long time. Have you ever searched for something that was lost for a very long time?

TEACHABLE MOMENT 7
Do you think it is a good idea to bring a pet into an Opera House? Were the animals on their best behavior? Where would your pet be welcome? Grandma's house? In school? At Mom and Dad's workplace?

TEACHABLE MOMENT 8
The opera singers have different voices. Is the Bass voice high or low? Is the Lyric-soprano voice high or low? Which voice is the lowest voice on the face of the earth?

TEACHABLE MOMENT 9
Is your voice high or low? Will it always be high or low? What kind of voices do your mother or father have? Is their voice high or low?

TEACHABLE MOMENT 10
Where and when do you sing? At home? At school? At church? At play?

Acknowledgements

Many thanks to Dr. Laura Apol,
Poet, Author, and Associate Professor of Children's Literature
in the College of Education at Michigan State University,
for her expertise in helping me refine Mariella's story.

And to Melanie Helton, Professor of Voice
and Director of MSU Opera Theatre,
whose guidance has brought
important authenticity to the storyline.
Her reference material about composers, concert halls,
voices, and instruments, gives parents and teachers
readily available information to guide discussions
about the "wonderful world of Opera".

APPENDIX

Explanation of Terms

An **Opera** is a big show in which all the words are put to music and sung by very beautiful, loud voices. The characters in the opera tell the audience a story. The stories of operas can be funny (comedies) or sad (tragedies).

An **Opera House** is a building used for opera performances consisting of a stage with scenery, an orchestra pit, audience seating, and places backstage for costumes and items used in the opera. In Europe, old-time opera houses may have six or seven levels of seating for the audience.

A **Concert Hall** is a large theatre which can be used for opera and symphony concerts, as well as solo recitals from both singers and instrumentalists.

An **Orchestra Pit** is a low area in front of the stage in which musicians perform.

A **Stage** is a large raised area where musicians perform and can be seen easily by the audience.

An **Aria** is a song sung by one voice in an opera.

Bravo is a form of applause when shouted by members of the audience at the end of an especially pleasing performance. Strictly speaking, "bravo" is for a single man, "brava" for a woman, and "bravi" for a group of performers.

Wonderful First Operas for Children:

The Magic Flute by Mozart; *Hansel and Gretel* by Engelbert Humperdinck; *Little Women* by Mark Adamo; *The Pirates of Penzance* by Gilbert & Sullivan.

Voices in the Opera

A *Tenor* has the highest voice of a male singer.

A *Lyric Soprano* has a warm, bright, high female voice.

A *Baritone* has a male voice lower than a Tenor.

A *Bass* has the lowest human voice on earth!

A *Mezzo Soprano* has a voice lower than a Lyric Soprano.

Musical Instruments of the Orchestra

The **string section** consists of violins, violas, cellos and double basses. They often play the melody.

The **percussion** make the rhythm of the opera and also can make lots of sound effects.

44

The **woodwinds** can include flute, oboe, English horn and clarinet. They often play variations on the melody. The flute is sometimes used as a solo instrument with the Lyric Soprano.

The **brass section** is made up of trumpets, trombones, French horns and tubas (oom-pah!). It often announces the arrival of the hero, usually the tenor.

The **harp** is used to portray something heavenly!

Inside Our Opera House

A Backdrops

Backdrops are usually made of heavy canvas material. Scenes are painted on each canvas. They are raised and lowered, changing the scenery to match the storyline of the opera.

B Mechanical Room for the Stage

This is what makes all that neat stuff possible.

C Storage Room and Elevator

Lots of costumes, music stands, chairs, and other furniture are stored here. The elevator brings this equipment to the stage level.

D Main Stage

The opera is performed here.

E Orchestra Pit

The conductor and instrumentalists play the music that accompanies the singers here.

F Storage

More storage space for costumes and beautiful hats.

G Seating

Opera houses may be very small and some are very large. Most people are seated in this main area.

H Box Seats

For a private and more spacious seating area, some patrons will enjoy these premium seats.

Some Composers of Opera

Tchaikovsky

May 7, 1840 – November 6, 1893

Peter Iylich Tchaikovsky was a Russian composer, who wrote the operas *Eugene Onegin* and *The Queen of Spades*, but also wrote the ballets *Sleeping Beauty* and *The Nutcracker*.

Rossini

February 29, 1792 – November 13, 1868

Gioachino Rossini was born into a family of musicians. He was singing, playing piano, and performing in church by the age of 10 years. His most famous opera is *The Barber of Seville* (in Italian, *Il Barbiere di Siviglia,* pronounced *Eel Barbeeairay dee Seeveelya!*).

December 22, 1858 –
November 29, 1924

Giacomo Puccini was an Italian composer best known for his operas, *Madame Butterfly, Tosca,* and *La Bohème.*

October 10, 1813 –
January 27, 1901

Giuseppe Verdi was an Italian composer of opera. He is best known for the operas *Aida, La Traviata* and *Rigoletto.*

January 27, 1756 –
December 5, 1791

Wolfgang Amadeus Mozart wrote his first symphony at the age of 8 years and his first opera at the age of 12. He was considered a child prodigy. His most famous operas are *The Marriage of Figaro* and *The Magic Flute.*

November 29, 1797 –
April 8, 1848

Gaetano Donizetti was born into a very poor family, but was musically trained and wrote church music and the famous operas *Lucia di Lammermoor* and *Don Pasquale.*

November 18, 1836 –
May 29, 1911

May 13, 1842 –
November 22, 1900

William Gilbert & Arthur Sullivan wrote lots of very, very funny operas for people in London and all over the world. *The Pirates of Penzance* and *H.M.S. Pinafore* are their most popular works.